AF584798

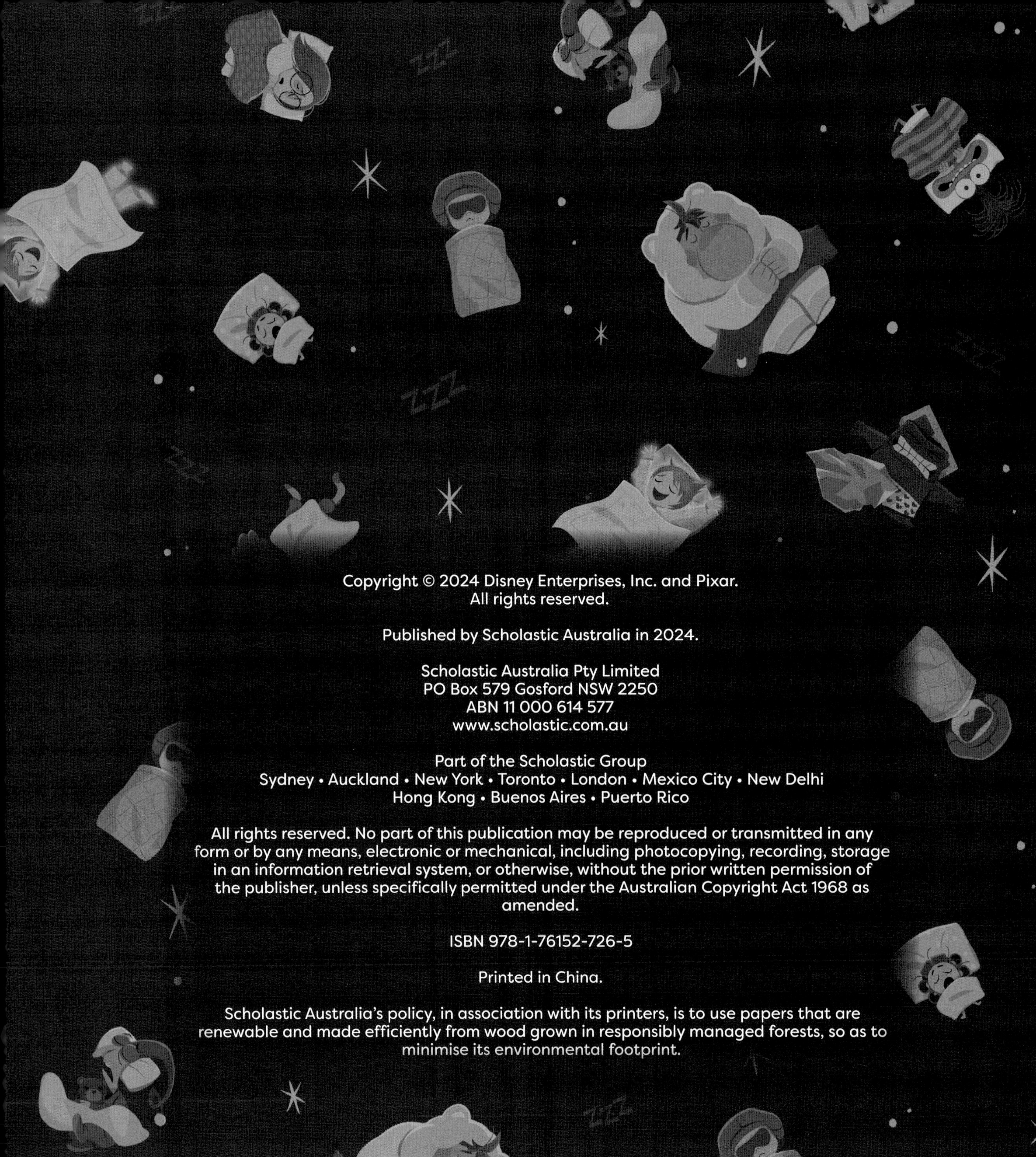

Copyright © 2024 Disney Enterprises, Inc. and Pixar.
All rights reserved.

Published by Scholastic Australia in 2024.

Scholastic Australia Pty Limited
PO Box 579 Gosford NSW 2250
ABN 11 000 614 577
www.scholastic.com.au

Part of the Scholastic Group
Sydney • Auckland • New York • Toronto • London • Mexico City • New Delhi
Hong Kong • Buenos Aires • Puerto Rico

All rights reserved. No part of this publication may be reproduced or transmitted in any form or by any means, electronic or mechanical, including photocopying, recording, storage in an information retrieval system, or otherwise, without the prior written permission of the publisher, unless specifically permitted under the Australian Copyright Act 1968 as amended.

ISBN 978-1-76152-726-5

Printed in China.

Scholastic Australia's policy, in association with its printers, is to use papers that are renewable and made efficiently from wood grown in responsibly managed forests, so as to minimise its environmental footprint.

Disney · PIXAR

INSIDE OUT 2

GO TO SLEEP, ANXIETY!

Written by **Luna Chi**

Illustrated by **Gurihiru**

SCHOLASTIC

SYDNEY AUCKLAND NEW YORK TORONTO LONDON MEXICO CITY
NEW DELHI HONG KONG BUENOS AIRES PUERTO RICO

It was bedtime at Headquarters!

While Riley was sleeping, her Emotions got ready for bed. They too needed to recharge for another day of fun.

Joy brushed her teeth for an extra-sparkly smile.

Sadness tucked in her stuffed animals.

Anger did some exercises to get a good night's rest.

And **Fear** always had on a night-light (or nine).

Even Riley's new Emotions had their own bedtime routines. **Envy** wanted to look pretty and rested for the day to come. **Embarrassment's** cosy pyjamas kept him feeling warm and safe, while bored **Ennui** mindlessly scrolled through her phone.

Now that everyone was ready, it was time for sleep!

Joy happily crawled into bed.

She was about to nod off when—

A commotion in Headquarters startled
everyone
out of bed.

Joy ran towards the noise. **Disgust** was supposed to be working the night shift behind the console. **What could've happened?**

It was **Anxiety!**

She **paced, worried, scribbled** and **worried some more.**

Anxiety wouldn't respond to anyone. **Anger** whipped out a megaphone. He and **Joy** leaned in . . .

Finally, she looked up.
'What's the matter?' Joy asked.
Anxiety let out a big sigh. **'I can't fall asleep.'**

'But you *have* to go to sleep!' Envy grumbled. 'I need my twelve hours of beauty rest if I want to look as good as Disgust!'

'I'm trying!' said Anxiety. 'But my worries spin around and around in my head . . . and then I even worry about not sleeping!'

The friends were ready to help. **Anger** suggested pull-ups. **'Twenty reps keeps you mean, lean and dreamin'.'**

Disgust offered up her aroma diffuser. **'It's minty!'**

Fear presented his favourite night-light. **'So you won't be scared of the dark!'**

Ennui, who didn't care about much, continued scrolling on her phone. **'Who needs sleep, anyway?'**

Embarrassment walked up to **Anxiety** and wrapped her in a squishy bear hug—but then **Envy** wanted one too.

Sadness began to read slowly from one of the Mind Manuals. While that was putting everyone else to sleep, **Anxiety** was still very much awake.

Joy quickly shut the book. **'I think I have an idea.'**

Joy knew **Anxiety** loved lists and counting. 'Why don't we try a little meditation? Can you list five things you're grateful for today?'

Anxiety glanced at everyone around her. She tried to think faster, but all that came to mind was . . .

I DON'T KNOW!
I DON'T KNOW!
I DON'T KNOW!
I DON'T KNOW!
I DON'T KNOW!

They needed a new idea. **Joy** grabbed a piece of paper from the cart.

She sat at a table and began working furiously.

She made an origami paper sculpture of herself!

'Sometimes when my mind is busy, and I have too many thoughts all at once . . . working with my hands helps me feel better.'

Anxiety leaned in for a closer look.

'Maybe this could help you too?' Joy asked.

Anxiety got to work.

A few hundred folds later . . .

. . . she was finally finished! **Anxiety** held out her little origami figure, and the rest of the Emotions cheered.

But suddenly, **Anxiety's** eyes filled with tears. 'Look how delicate it is! It could be *crushed* before tomorrow!'

She began to spiral again.

Joy was startled. 'No, no, no, it'll be okay—'

'You're right,' Sadness chimed in. 'That *could* happen.' She gently patted Anxiety on the back. 'What would you do if it got crushed?'

Anxiety stopped panicking to think. 'I guess I would have to throw it away.

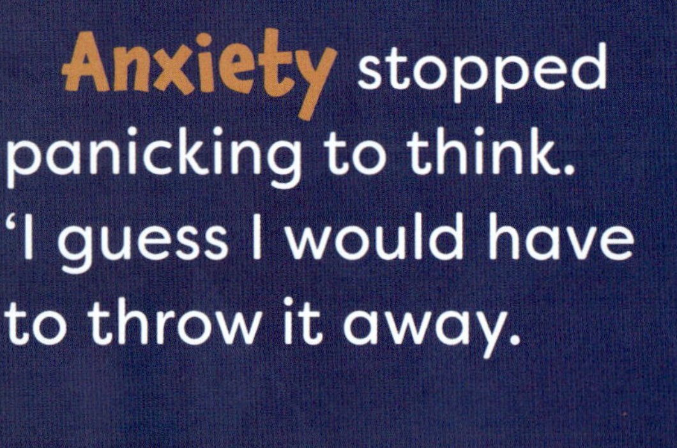

'But then I could build a new one. Maybe with even sturdier paper.

'And I could fix the mistakes I made today.' **Anxiety** smiled. 'Thank you, **Sadness.** I feel better when I have a plan.'

Anxiety let out a big yawn. 'Maybe I could make origami figures of Riley, and Mum and Dad too . . .' Her eyelids began to grow heavy, but she continued folding more paper.

Disgust returned to the console while the other Emotions went to bed.

Everyone was ready to sleep.
'Lights out!' **Joy** said once more.

At long last, all was well. The Emotions were cosy in bed, peacefully dreaming of the day ahead.

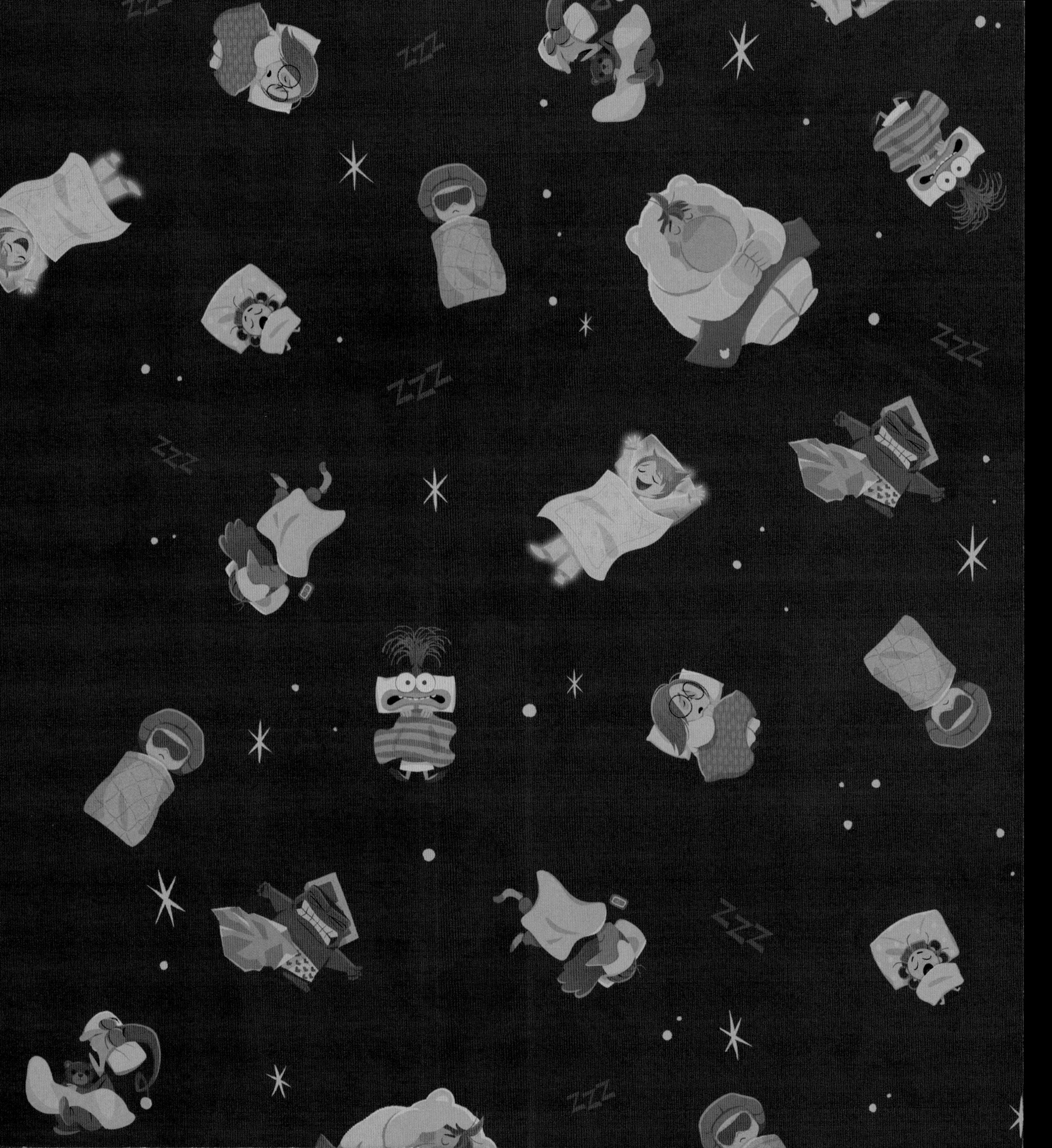